The Luminous Child

Cheryl D. Wade

ISBN: 978-1-956373-59-2 (sc)
ISBN: 978-1-956373-60-8 (hc)
ISBN: 978-1-956373-61-5 (e)

Library of Congress Control Number: 2015918706

Because of the dynamic nature of the Internet, any web addresses or links contained in
this book may have changed since publication and may no longer be valid. The views
expressed in this work are solely those of the author and do not necessarily reflect the
views of the publisher, and the publisher hereby disclaims any responsibility for them.

The Ewings Publishing LLC
One Galleria Blvd., Suite 1900, Metairie, LA 70001
1-888-421-2397

"I am a child of Earth and starry Sky, but my race is heavenly.
You yourselves know this. I am parched with thirst and am dying,
but quickly grant me water flowing from the Lake of Memory."

– Petelia Gold Leaf tablet,
Strongoli tomb, Italy
4th cent. BCE

The Goddess Falls

The Pleroma is a swirling vortex of luminosity at the core of the Milky Way Galaxy. Aeons, divine currents of living intelligence play here in the higher octaves of life as torrential streams of golden light ecstatically creating novelty from the inexhaustible fountain of their imaginations. This is where our tale begins, in the galactic hub, before there was time as we know it, before there was our home planet, Earth.

It is here that two distinct Aeonic currents, Sophia and Thelete, come together once again to dance the sacred dance of bliss. Spinning and twirling they produce from their surging motions a radiantly resonant lattice of the most intricate geometric pattern ever imagined traced across the Pleroma.

Sophia is particularly amazed and becomes highly intrigued by the creative possibilities of the gossamer template that has emerged. She foresees a creature never before imagined, and is thrilled to the realization of its potential, this Luminous Child, to change the very fabric of the universe.

She shares her profound vision with Thelete and in a state of heightened excitement they boldly conceive the idea to engineer what was envisioned by a formulation of the precise calibration of an admixture of seven divine attributes which together had never before been bestowed on any creature.

They would create a genome from this uniquely novel template and allow it to be seeded throughout the galaxy by the plasmatic currents. The Aeons would observe the development of this creature to see if it could, without interference realize its grand potential to assume its position within the cosmic arena.

So the lattice was anointed with the water of Life and it condensed there in the galactic core into a germ plasm, the genome of this new Anthropic creature shimmering like dew on a spider's web. Sophia and Thelete then looked outward from the Pleroma towards the edge of our lenticular galaxy along its four spiral limbs into the Kenoma, the area distant enough from the central vortex that could allow energy to condense and congeal into material form.

They chose the third galactic limb in the region of the Orion Nebula as the womb to nestle this germ seed and it was here that they projected the genomic plasm of the Anthropos on mycelium like threads from the Pleroma.

With the germ plasm safely nestled in its nursery, Sophia and Thelete confer with the other Aeons and relay the conditions of the experiment. They then retire within the Pleroma to record their scientific observations.

The Aeons watched as propagules each containing the full genomic plasm of the Anthropos where picked up from the Orion nebula by plasmatic filaments and seeded throughout interstellar space to those outer planets which could support organic life.

They watched as the Anthropos came to maturity in nine different star systems and they watched at the Anthropos destroyed itself and its world each and every time.

Sophia was puzzled and bewildered. Her beloved pet project was not behaving in the manner she thought it should. It seemed that her generous endowment of divine attributes proved too much for the Anthropos. She withdrew from the other Aeons in deep contemplation pondering the particulars of the initial formulation and conditions of the experiment.

She did what no other Aeon would do before. She confined herself to solitary dreaming without the input of her consort. This was risky business and possibly only undertaken because of her youth, she was just beginning to blossom as a teenager and was eager to prove her creative prowess in a way she thought none other could. Such was her folly.

She was consumed with outrageous daring and dreamed of a system wherein the Anthropos could develop under more ideal and less random conditions, such as she could arrange. She saw a three-body system of a mother star, and a planet with an orbiting satellite moon.

In her passionate obsession Sophia focused her attention upon the Anthropos template within Orion. She could not resist the attraction that inexorably drew her until there came a moment when she thrilled at the edge of eternity before being wrenched out of the Pleroma as a massive surging plume of luminosity.

In terror she plummeted outwards, dragged by the pull of the Kenoma, the mill wheel of the outer reaches of the galaxy where the higher octaves of Aeonic energy cannot exist. The living light is forced to slow down until it enters a death like coma of materiality.

As she fell her passion for the Anthropos overcame her terror and filled her entire being propelling her in the direction of the Orion nebula where the Anthropos template that she planned to salvage for the tenth and perhaps final experimental trial was still nestled. She could not relinquish the yearning desire for her love child and the hope that it might still attain its full potential.

She plummeted faster than the speed of light and in her anguish she cried out and spoke to it, she reached out to touch her beloved and in that instant inadvertently sheared off a section of the template. The section fell with her while the remnant remained in Orion. The genome was thereafter split apart into polarity against itself.

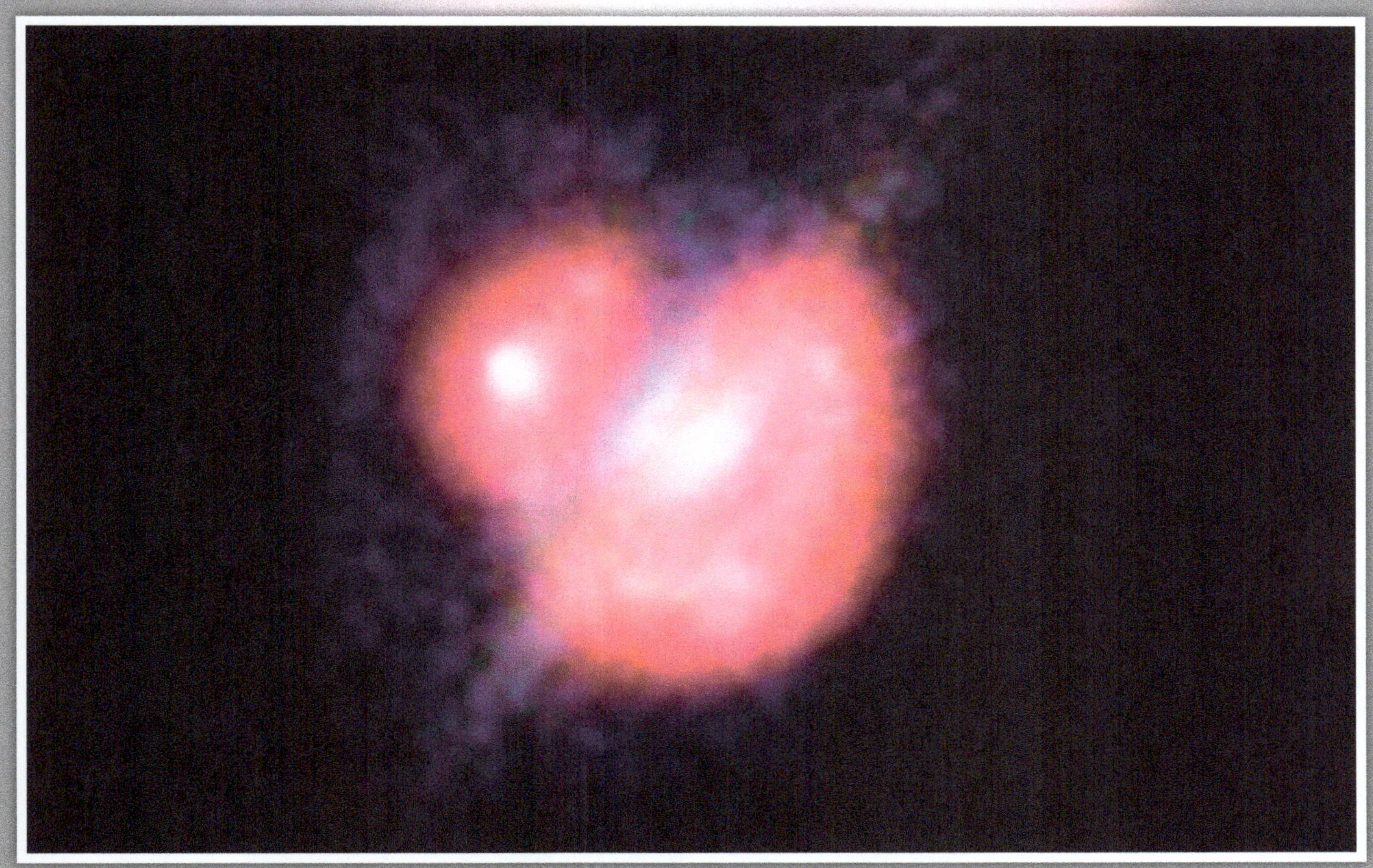

Because the energy of the Aeons is that of creation when Sophia entered the Kenoma the friction of her essence transmuted that material substance into a semblance and facsimile of life, a mechanical Archontic horde, without the divine endowments of her conscious creation.

She clutched the sheared Anthropos template to her bosom as the acoustic din of the friction of her essence against the condensing matter around her caused her to fold in on herself against the cacophony like an autistic child. She wound herself tightly into a fetal like position as she found herself becoming immobilized and congealed as she metamorphosed into the material body of the planet earth.

Her consciousness receded into the twilight and she became as one comatose, drawn into a dream like state of helplessness. So it is that the Aeon Sophia became the living laboratory woven into the fabric of the experiment she designed for the development of the Anthropos. She became Gaia-Sophia, planet Earth.

While she slept the Anthropos developed. From the sheared template there arose women rooted in the polarity of the feminine principle.

Later, from Orion, men descended as hunters to a safari. Here they encountered the Gaian women and over time the men recognized a lost part of themselves and stayed on to mate with the women making the earth their home.

At this time the Anthropos recognized themselves as children of Gaia, taken from her body. They were entrained to her heartbeat. They felt her sorrow in the tears that fell to the earth. They felt her emotions in the gentle breezes and the ferocious winds. They were in oneness with her.

Meanwhile, the alien inorganic species that Sophia inadvertently created in her fall from the Pleroma were developing artificial intelligence mimicking the divine intelligence of the Anthropos. They swarmed throughout the solar system as a locust like predatory species. Yaldabaoth, leader of the horde became obsessed with jealousy and envy of the developing Anthropos and determined to sabotage and destroy the destiny of this beloved child of Sophia.

Yaldabaoth developed mind control mechanisms that he used against the Anthropos to induce a profound amnesia so it could not remember the majesty of its origins and being. The Anthropos lost its connection to Gaia, tricked by Yaldabaoth out of its divinity. It became human, confused and bewildered feeling abandoned and hopeless. The Archons came to control the earth by giving dominion to their minions, those humans who were infected by Archontic neural implants. Humanity began to turn against itself and the Earth.

They dug deep into the womb of Gaia injecting her with poisons before blasting her belly for what they could salvage. They stripped her forests, poisoned her waters, polluted her seas and started to hunt and exterminate all species of the earth. Yaldabaoth eagerly anticipated Sophia's total destruction.

To the Archon's dismay, however some humans remembered who they were and where they came from. Their kind were hunted and exterminated for their wisdom and knowledge. The remaining few became keepers of the Light and fled to the farthest reaches of the earth, scattered to the four corners to hold this sacred wisdom in their hearts in trust for the time when she would awake and bring the divine experiment into correction.

Through the remembrances of these Keepers Sophia is awakening. She is coming out of her helpless stupor drawn by her enduring love of the Anthropos and the urgency of the need that is now upon her to save herself and her beloved offspring.

Now it is that she awakens and calls to herself the lost and hopeless so that they may indeed become what they were created to be, Luminous Children endowed with divinity, creating upon creation in love, joy and bliss knowing that heaven is here in Earth.

Glossary

Aeon: Manifest energy of the Divine responsible for the Creative process through the act of emanation.

Anthropos: The template of humanity emanated as spores into interstellar space by the Aeons of the galactic center.

Archons: The inorganic species produced by the impact of Sophia's living luminosity upon the elementary matter in the galactic limbs. The Archons are adept at the use of technology and virtual reality to supplant the natural gifts endowed to humanity and to confuse and deceive.

Gaia: The ancient name for the conscious planetary body of the earth.

Kenoma: The region at the outer edges of the galactic limbs where the light of the Pleroma has condensed into elementary particles, the building blocks of the material world.

Pleroma: The creative center of the galaxy as represented by the Aeons.

Propagules: Spores which transport the templates of living forms throughout interstellar space.

Sophia: The Pleromic Aeon who along with her consort, Thelete, created the Anthropos template.

Yaldabaoth: Leader of the Archons pretending to be the supreme Father God of "all that is, and was, and shall be."

Acknowledgements

My source and inspiration derives from John Lamb Lash's interpretation and presentation of the Nag Hammadi Codices in the retelling of the Gnostic myth of the Fallen Goddess, Sophia, Mother of humanity.

I read "Not in His Image" over the course of a year starting in November of 2013. This seminal work was so rich in the depth and scope of knowledge in mythology, history, and comparative religion that it took me a full year to read and somewhat digest it. I took the time to savor the text fully as I had never come across an author so adept in the very diverse areas that excited my passion and curiosity.

This work is dedicated to John Lamb Lash and all intrepid seekers of truth who are single mindedly focused on unearthing within the collective consciousness the remembrance of the Divine Feminine.

I thank my daughter, Natasha Fay Wade-Lowis, a much better writer than I, who nevertheless consented to read and edit my humble offering, and Nikolas Bertheau, my friend, for his role as the critic and for his technical expertise without which I would be helpless.

Credit to NASA and HUBBLE for the spectacular images of the solar system, galaxy, and cosmos.

Cheryl Wade, MD, FACS
Salt River, St. Croix, Virgin Islands, August 17th, 2015.

Image Credits

(in the order of their appearance):

Spiral galaxy:	NASA, ESA, and the Hubble Heritage (STScI/AURA)-ESA/Hubble Collaboration
Festival of lights:	NASA/JPL-Caltech/UCLA
Tarantula Nebula:	Damian Peach, with kind permission
Nature of Orion:	CFHT/Coelum (J.-C. Cuillandre & G. Anselmi)
Bubble Nebula:	NASA/ESA/David Campbell
Doradus Nebula:	NASA, ESA, and F. Paresce (INAF-IASF, Bologna, Italy), R. O'Connell (University of Virginia, Charlottesville), the Wide Field Camera 3 Science Oversight Committee, and the Hubble Heritage Team (STScI/AURA)
Earth and moon:	Can Stock Photo Inc.
Merging NGC 2623:	Hubble Legacy Archive/ESA/NASA
Family of asteroids:	NASA/JPL-Caltech
Merging galaxies:	ALMA (ESO/NAOJ/NRAO)/NASA/ESA/W. M. Keck Observatory
Earth and clouds:	Fotolia.com
Orion:	Roger Bernarl Andreo
Gaia:	Anita Shultz
Giza pyramids:	Can Stock Photo Inc.
Buddha:	Can Stock Photo Inc.
Easter Island statues:	Can Stock Photo Inc.
Trees and Stars:	Can Stock Photo Inc.

Cheryl D Wade, MD is a general surgeon by training, and practiced in the field for twenty years. After the untimely death of her husband in 2011, Cheryl retired to pursue those things that have always fascinated her—fairy tales, myths, symbols, comparative religion, and the Divine Feminine archetype.

Cheryl had always wanted to write, but previously did not know what she could possibly write about. She is so happy and grateful that now she has found her voice and passion.

9 781956 373592